Kachanga
Goticos

SASH

PUBLISHED BY FOREL BOOKS

COVER ILLUSTRATION BY SASH

ISBN-13: 978-0615442365

ISBN-10: 0615442366

The Kachanga Goticos in . . .

"A Question of Succession"

In an absurdly faraway time known as "right now" (but not quite) and in a ludicrously faraway place called "right here" (sort of), there is a world quite similar to our own but in which our rules would seem very silly. Not quite a parallel universe, but a diagonal one. A world where sinister cuteness and earnest hypocrisy perpetually vie for supremacy. O, the vanity of it all!

I

An immense flying jellyshark, menacing and scowling, inches its way towards Jixim, who stands transfixed and spouting little beads of sweat. And then, surprising even himself by the sudden gesture, Jixim hugs the creature, whose attitude just as suddenly inverts. Becoming touched by Jixim's hug, it trembles out a large beaded teardrop, and then skips away into the distance, going "Yip! Yip! Yip!"

A young girl's voice asks, "Are you proud of yourself?"

Jixim turns around slowly, perhaps thinking it's a trick, but sees a pretty, white-gold-haired young lady. "I showed it love," he offers in the way of explanation.

She smiles a sweetly mocking smile, perhaps out of her depth, perhaps not. "How would you like to show *me* some? Hmm?"

Jixim feels the challenge. A kid-glove challenge, but a challenge still. He approaches her, all the while staring her down. She becomes nervous. He hugs her, facing her still. They embrace for a few seconds, long as any lengthy thing. She falls down on her knees and cries.

The pressure begins to ease out with the tears. Soon, composure is regained . . . at a generous price.

She looks up at him, hands and knees still on the ground. "You're Jixim, are you not? I've seen you around."

"Yes, we have a friend in common."

"It's strange. . . ."

Jixim's sense is sharply distracted by a fleeting shadow. He looks up. "Look! The Vulture!"

"Don't move!" she blurts out.

"No, he's alright."

The Vulture's shadow is cast over them as he swoops down. Soon he stands in front of them. "I'm looking for Jixim. Have you seen him?"

Jixim, who now radiates an utterly different persona, coolly answers, "No. If I do, what should I tell him?"

"Why, that the Vulture is looking for him, of course."

"Fine, if I see him, I'll tell him."

"Thank you."

The Vulture flies away.

Jixim resumes his typical attitude. The girl is puzzled.

"Why didn't you tell him you were you, Jixim?"

"To make this game more fun. The eye of the Vulture is not as keen as the Eagle's eye since the Vulture only looks for death and ignores the living. I think he wants help finding the guilty party."

"Guilty party? Guilty of what?"

"I don't know. But now I want to find out."

A familiar voice from somewhere: "Wait, Jixim, I'll tell you what."

Jixim and the *femme natale* in startled chorus: "Biendoror!"

The strange, though not discomfiting, presence of Biendoror is known to invigorate. "Of course. Hereta, you look as though you have only recently met Jixim. But that is not so bad. Anyway, this is the news: Somebody sent the Emperor an anonymous scorpion, who then bit him. The venom is quite active, shall we say?"

"And the Vulture?" asks Jixim.

"Probably only wants to know if it's mortal. He

could care less about finding the guilty party . . . "

". . . Because it's him."

"No, no, no! No."

"It *is* him."

"Remember, the Vulture can't kill. He has to await the mortification of another's flesh or their death, whichever comes first."

"But the Vulture has an agent, a representative," Hereta adds. "He may know things."

Jixim nods. "Yes, I say we go to him!"

"Ridiculous! With what pretext?" Biendoror wants to know.

"None," Jixim answers with a leer. "But with much in the way of *pretense.*"

"Then I'm sold," concludes Biendoror. "Let us go immediately by decidedly ignoring space and all its little stupidities."

II

They appear in the office of the Vulture's agent, a crony-crone who sits at his desk, furiously absorbed in his work. Furious yet not without pleasure of a sort. They see him but it's not mutual.

Jixim: "So . . . you're the Vulture's confidante?"

The agent sits up straight, rather composed considering the surprise intrusion. "Who the Hades are you? How did you get in?"

Jixim smiles slightly. "Now, now. The Vulture and I spoke. Very pleasant. He was looking for Jixim and Jixim wants to know for what ends."

"Ah. Jixim the Changeling. You are one of his?"

"Mm-hm."

The agent looks at the assembled trio, and half-sighs. "The Emperor has been stung by an eight-legged pest. If the Caesar dies, the Vulture will consume him, as is his duty. But will he too then die by dint of a venomous carcass? The Vulture is no Phoenix and is entitled to his concerns."

Biendoror interjects, "But the Imperial Eucharist must be devoured. It has always been decreed."

The agent looks at him blankly. "What can I say? The Vulture is becoming vain in his age."

Hereta huffs. "What I want to know is, who cares?" She looks at Jixim and whispers, for everyone else to hear it, "Jixim, let's go to the night's candy-lit shore and have feelings of one another."

Jixim makes note of the request and all its touching implications, but . . . "Yes, my pet, my mascot. Only that is too simple and safe for now. At this juncture, I need to delve into complicating my attention."

The agent looks surprised. "You are Jixim, then?"

Biendoror: "Heroism. Adventure. Correct?"

Jixim nods. "More or less. More, in fact."

"Will anyone listen?" asks the flustered agent.

"Love is an adventure," counters Hereta.

"Hmm . . ." Jixim thinks that one through.

The agent stands up behind his desk. "May I remind you, Jixim, that if my client doesn't eat the Emperor's flesh with love, it won't be a sacrament and the succession will fail and with it all the levels of the realm?"

"It *could* cause chaos in the negative sense," confirms Biendoror.

Jixim affects a morose stance. "And it's my job to allay everyone's fears? To assure that bird a delectable meal?"

The agent looks offended. "As a mage, aren't you—?"

Jixim nods to Biendoror, who nods back: "Looks like our work here is done."

III

They are outdoors once again.

Jixim protests, "All this talk of politics frazzles me."

Hereta brushes his cheek. "Why do they all think you can help?"

Biendoror smirks to himself. "As alchemical engineer, Jixim can change any substance, not just himself. For example, poison into wine."

"Yummy. And you, Biendoror?"

"I only see the folly in measurements such as time and space."

"Can't you go to the Imperial Palace and help, then? Jixim and I want to be alone."

Biendoror bristles slightly. "I'm miffed. I'll leave you alone. But I won't help. It doesn't work that way."

"You're right!" states Jixim. "I received a message from my soul to not do anything about this predicament, so-called!"

Biendoror walks up to him. "Comrades to the end." They shake hands warmly. Biendoror disappears, saying simply, "I am away!"

IV

Biendoror is in the nether state between static space and the artifice of seasons. He thinks, "Maybe I should go to the Imperial City and see for myself how the bureaucrats are mismanaging the whole affair."

In this unperceived state, he enters the Palace and sees the Scorpion approaching the Emperor and stinging him. The frightened Emperor exclaims, "Ow!

Digestive waste!" Biendoror affirms, "That's yester-day."

Biendoror sees several ministers gathered around the sick Emperor. One minister gravely intones, "He is on fire. His blood is like corrosive acid. His face is like a model for the Jolly Roger." Biendoror affirms, "That's tomorrow."

Floating to another room in the Palace, he sees the Vulture sitting and talking with an official: "My esquire just told me that Jixim and his friends came and went. The self-same which I met!"

"If the meat gets stuck in your craw, the land is doomed," answers the official.

"I don't want to die," sighs the Vulture.

"You? What about my house?"

Biendoror affirms, "And that's today."

In the nether, various sprites, aliens and other "travelers" swirl around him. He judges the palatial situation: "A mess of delirious fineness. The best kind."

V

A palace guard announces, "The Princess has decided to make her entrance! Whoops, there she is."

The Princess walks in silently, with a haughty reserve, very ornately attired, uppercrusty, and with servants. She sits in her throne, with a man at either foot down on the floor licking and sucking devotedly.

"There is fear spreading with the news," the Princess says to the chief dignitary, from whom she often solicits counsel.

"Yes, your tortured overwrought highness."

"What is my father's bill of health?"

"Poor, mademoiselle."

"What is to become of us all?"

"No one knows. This has never occurred in all the aeons. The succession an unbroken chain. And now this Scorpion most mysterious. As well as his master's identity."

"Assuming he doesn't have self-mastery."

"The Scorpion is too low."

The princess ponders curiously. "So who is high enough?"

"Anyone that doesn't crawl on the ground may master themselves."

"What about the Vulture or the Eagle? What about the Pelican?"

"The Eagle and the Pelican have absolute self-mastery and so are above reproach. The Vulture . . ."

"Yes? Yes?"

". . . has nothing to gain and everything to lose in such a crime. It may be anyone who directed the

Scorpion."

"And this Scorpion is not to be found?"

"No, your-highness-is-my-lowness. Though dependent, he is shrewd."

"Should I call on Vatvoy?"

"The great hedonist seer? The Princess must understand that he could cause as much trouble as he repaired. Too unfathomable. I wouldn't recommend it."

"In that case, I will call him. He makes me feel reality." In a loud voice: "Guards, summon Vatvoy to me!"

"Yes, your ascendancy!" answers the head guard with a snapping salute.

There is immediately a glowing outburst of flame in the middle of the vast throne room. Out of it steps Vatvoy, who wears an oversized turban somewhat covering and shading over his eyes. He has four legs instead of the customary two. Everyone is stunned at his impromptu entrance.

"Just call me a tetrapede," he suggests to no one in particular. Everyone watches silently. Vatvoy smiles. "My eyes are in darkness that they may appeal to the Light."

He walks up to a guard, and holds his left hand in front of the sentry's nervous face. "Kiss my finger." The guard uncertainly kisses it. "Now I'll kiss yours."

The guard dutifully offers his finger, which Vatvoy kisses.

"Now get out!" Vatvoy shouts. The guard is so taken aback that he proceeds to leave, even without formal orders from his monarch. Vatvoy calls out after him, "Go smell a rose or something! Wear two helmets!" The guard exits.

Vatvoy grins. "And why not? It might fortify his resolve. He shouldn't have paid me any attention."

The chief dignitary looks on disapprovingly. "This is silly, a travesty."

Vatvoy looks at him. "You, come here. Kiss my finger."

"Don't be a fool," replies the dignitary in a measured tone.

"No, sir. Of course not. He who is bad is a fool. And he who is good is twice the fool. But he who is above such things is the grandmaster of all fools. Good lord!"

The dignitary is stonily silent.

Vatvoy scratches his head. "Right. Now where am I?"

"The Imperial Palace," answers the Princess.

"Oh, yes. And you are the Princess. I prescribe that you and I drink each other's liquid life essences on one of your precious orange cushions. Say, after this meeting is over?"

The Princess blushes a little.

The dignitary intervenes. "Vatvoy, you have been called here for assistance during this renowned crisis which may annihilate our entire sphere. . . . Or do you want the universal empire to vanish?"

"Can you help, Vatvoy?" asks the Princess.

"There is nothing to do. Whatever happens is perfect. It is always so."

"Some seer," chortles the dignitary.

"I see you," replies Vatvoy. "And I would like to kiss you. But you won't let me, especially not in court."

"I see that you are, at best, ineffectual. At worst, quite mad."

"Who is seeing what? Have you ever seen the pink puma? Or the alphabet of crystal melons? Or the glittering hell for mean people?"

"Of course not."

"No? Good. Wait, it's not good. You, sir, have no imagination!" Vatvoy begins to weep. "I can't even speak with you. Please leave. Curse you. Please . . . go. I love you."

The princess signals for the chief dignitary to go. He shrugs and exits.

"Thank the great Solamander that the five-sided cube has left!" announces Vatvoy cheerfully.

"Vatvoy, is there anything that you can do?" the Princess inquires.

"My dear, dear heart . . . how can I do when I don't even be? Now come, the only thing is to not stay here but to attend to your private salon."

He cups each of her breasts fondlingly. "Yes," he confirms, "let us retire." He offers her his arm, and she takes it. They walk out together.

VI

A night scene, with a snowy cityscape. The buildings in this part of town are of the Culinary school of architecture and accordingly shaped like various types of food, a gigantic table with tablecloth, glazed fruits, etc. In one apartment, there is a party. Jixim and Hereta are there, but standing apart from the festivities, watching.

A man with a spyglass looks out the window. "It's snowing seven-pointed flakes tonight. My favorite!"

Hereta looks restless. "Oh, Tinshalu!" she calls out. "Can you bring me that glass of wormwood wine?"

"Certainly," he responds. He brings her the glass and goes off.

Jixim projects a pensive air. "The mood in the city remains much the same," he offers casually.

Hereta's answer is independent. "All the talk here has been about how injust it is for the slaves. That we shouldn't have slaves anymore. No one cares about the Emperor's plight."

"A slave is only someone who hasn't freed themselves."

"Yes, but their life is all burden. Look at them down there."

Jixim looks out the window and notes the downtrodden zombies hauling things about.

"Perhaps," he muses, "the free people want a change. It may be the time for one."

"The slaves can't tell the difference between their state and ours?" Hereta asks.

"How can they? They barely live. They only *think* they live."

Suddenly, a man begins addressing the group. "Everyone, I have an announcement! You all know of the predicament which menaces our orderly plane. The Emperor's body is poison and how this will affect the Vulture and the consecration of the next Emperor is unknown."

He continues. "If the Vulture dies, he won't shit out, as it were, a new Emperor. Without such a personification of our domain, who are we? Or even, can we be?"

The man pauses, and then adds: "Which is why I offer that we revolt for the slaves and free them! There is nothing to forsake!"

The guests second him with, "Yea! Here here! Here there!"

Jixim is aghast. He lunges a step or two and quickly addresses the crowd. "Fools! Know you not that no one enslaves the slaves? That each slave is simultaneously prisoner, prison and warden? Thus, only a slave can free himself."

Everyone looks and listens quietly. "Further," he continues, "there is no shame in slavery. For it seasons freedom once this is gained!"

"The servant is the master in disguise," opines a guest.

"So now you remember," answers Jixim. "Be quick not to forget it again!"

"If you would truly be kind to a slave, let him alone!" exclaims another guest.

"Yes," Jixim says.

Another guest pipes up, "Maybe plant a seed, give him fertilizer and instructions, but let him tend her own garden."

"Quite so," acknowledges Jixim with some satisfaction.

The original speaker man who would have started

a veritable Reign of Error appears relieved the crowd of revellers has shown their forgiveness of him by promptly ignoring his presence. "Whew! I could go for some opium potato chips."

A voice answers, "Go for them before they come for you!"

Jixim and Hereta in chorus, as is their wont on such occasions, "Biendoror!"

"How is it?" inquires Jixim.

"Vatvoy's on the job. The Princess just commissioned him."

"Oh, like he's so helpful."

"Will he cast another toe jam spell?" Hereta asks.

"I don't think so," replies Biendoror. "Anyway, the Emperor will die very soon. And with him, perhaps everything."

"The Vulture's composure must be scanty," Jixim speculates.

"Earlier," Hereta informs Biendoror, "there were rumblings about giving the slaves freedom, but Jixim gave them a wonderful talk."

"They're bored and scared," Biendoror states matter-of-factly as he glances at the partyers. "That's when the truth gets jilted."

"The cads! I had to restore them."

"Jixim," Hereta says softly, "all that work you did

made me want to relax. Let's go to my sector."

"Fine. Biendoror?"

"No, you two go. I'll just sneak my way about, which is what I did tomorrow."

VII

Jixim and Hereta stand holding hands in front of a rocky night shore. The waves are splashing and curving up. In the air float geometric lamps that look like incandescent beehives.

"You see the shore? The vast waters?" Jixim asks.

"Yes, Jixim."

"That body of water means it doesn't matter what happens. Do you understand?"

"I think so."

"No."

"I understand."

"Then look," he says as he floats up in the air, and turns around to see her eyes.

Hereta is puzzled. "How?"

"The waters reflect moonlight. And moonlight is but reflected sunlight. And sunlight in turn. . . . If you see with the eye of the Eagle, what matters how well a buzzard sees? You will never want or go hungry. The carrion eaters will feast off your leftovers."

She gently floats up to him. They embrace. She is on a par with him.

"You can take love now," he says.

"I can make love now."

They stay locked in embrace above the dark waters. A giant anemone pops out calmly through the water's surface.

VIII

Biendoror is in a crime-slave slum. He is in his *imperceptible* mode. "Perhaps," he thinks, "a slave or servant has made do with venomology lately and cavorted with the Scorpion of Disgust."

He goes into a seedy, shadow-flecked bar and floats over to the even-darker back room. He sees a familiar figure holding forth to a small group of slave thugs.

"The Bat!" Biendoror exclaims to himself.

"If you all follow me," the Bat promises, "we'll be the masters. With all the confusion and loss, everyone will be scared. The Palace and the Police Temple will be easy to take."

"I might have known," thinks Biendoror. "Oh, but it doesn't matter."

"Something's changed here," says the Bat. "I sense it."

"Uh-oh. Better go." Biendoror leaves.

"Hmm . . ." the Bat ponders.

"What?" asks one of the thugs.

"Never mind."

IX

A huge news head (about twenty feet tall), decked with elaborate vestments and decor, declaims: "The Imperial One is dead. He was stung by an abysmal arachnid, and he was very old besides! His last words were:

(The effete Emperor is shown speaking from his emperor-size bed.) 'I suppose it seems odd. I see every moment afresh, with the innocence and formlessness of a new-born, and simultaneously am jaded and world-weary.'"

The head continues: "The event we have all await-ed is to be today at X hours in the Palacium. Be sure to see it! It may be the end of all! Oh, well! So much for lineage and the transmission of life! Maybe! May the Condorish One eat with composure and *digest.* If he *dies* it's no *jest!* Ah, I am truly sorry."

X

X marks the moment. A vast throng is in attendance at the Palacium, which is an immense open-air arena. The Princess and her court sit on a round dais in the very center of the arena. The Vulture—tense—sits nearby on a little volcano-like mound in a rock garden of sorts.

He rises and speaks: "Since, according to tradition immemorial, no one else can talk until I eat, allow me to state that in all the ages my wings have never been clipped and I have served well. And I love you all more than even I know! To her exaltedness, the Princess, I say, 'If this fails, I do Apollogize.' You are, at any rate, Empress stuff so far as I see. And now I taste."

All watch in frozen suspense. Some meditate anxiously. Jixim, Biendoror, and Hereta look on quietly, having well-situated seats.

The Vulture takes a piece of Emperor and places it in his mouth and swallows. He stands stiffly. And waits.

After a short while, he announces, "I ate the requisite piece. Nothing happens. No annihilation, we all live, but no new Emperor fertilized either."

The people murmur their ambivalence and confusion.

A diplomat spits, "Why, this is unheard of. This . . ."

". . . is sublime, buffoon boy of baboon quality," states Vatvoy.

Everyone is shocked as they suddenly notice Vatvoy's appearance. He smoothly walks across the dais.

He addresses the court and the multitude. "Everyone, hello is gone. From now on, you say heaveno. Much nicer, yes? Well, well!"

The throng looks perplexed.

"Allow me to explain to you who use your minds so much." He pauses momentarily and continues. "Everything is simply delightful! But why is all not death? For the Vulture looked quite nauseous and distressed. Perhaps he wanted candy instead! Oh, most foul the meat with scorpion toxin. Deadly. You all know that!"

An audience member shouts out, "Vatvoy, explain!"

Vatvoy glares. "Silence, dog! You would steal my timing!" He smiles. "Now, as I was saying, there is a new covenant. For the Princess and I made love so that nothing would happen."

"This ought to be good," offers Jixim.

"Don't count on it," counters Biendoror.

"It occurred to me. . . ." Vatvoy explains, "Why should our universal section perish? Let it perish when the great Vatvoy is no longer in it! So with the Princess I cast the null spell. I am number one. The Princess, a woman, is minus one—a minus in that she lies horizontally while my one wand stands vertically. Well, one plus minus one is nothing. So nothing happens."

"Princess, is it true you were defiled by Vatvoy?" a minister asks.

"Oh, yes," replies the Princess.

"I'm not sure," ponders the minister. "Is this an outrage?"

"Understand or serve," Vatvoy states.

"Oh, ha ha. I get it, of course," assures the minister.

"So I'm no longer necessary?" asks the Vulture.

"Of course not, bird," answers Vatvoy.

"Wild," the Vulture says quietly, with a tinge of disappointment.

Vatvoy caresses the Princess—now the Empress—and then cups the undersides of her breasts with his hands. "All fertility shall emanate through here from now onwards. The Empress! And the little Eaglets!"

The crowd cheers.

"Now," suggests Vatvoy, "Someone should give a great speech reminding you all to live for there is naught else to do! Will anyone listen?"

Vatvoy begins doing a calisthenic dance and gradually dances his way off the dais, disappearing down the stairs under the stage. The people are at first joyed, perhaps thinking he'll return momentarily, and then are surprised to find his exit not an act.

A minister arises and shouts, "All hail the Empress!" The crowd hails.

"I still say it's all politics," says Jixim.

"But do you feel a change in the aether?" asks Biendoror.

XI

Vatvoy is alone, elsewhere. His expression is an enigma. "Oh, my poor children! I told them the truth for their ears. But I'm a mocker! I neglected to tell them that *nothing* is infinitely greater than *everything!* Oh, Vatvoy! Ha ha! 'Nothing happens'! Ha ha! Ha ha ha!"

"The Ones And The Others"

Our heroes—such as they are—notice a change occurring. This change is of a very particular sort. It feels like life itself is being overthrown. On the one hand, nothing is the same; yet, on the other hand, nothing is different. But since nothing by definition does not exist, what can it matter? Very good! But just now Jixim and Biendoror are getting summoned to attend a testing of dubious people—free people in danger of falling into slavery. And it had started as such a promising day. . . .

I

"Hey, Biendoror," Jixim says, "There's a test happening at Central Thoroughfare."

"Lord, not again."

"Yeah, the Police Commander announced that those who are dubious, or who have fallen into dubiousness, must report there at M hours."

"Why is he so bored?" Biendoror wonders.

"Personally, I think he's trying to impress the Empress. They say he has a strawberry crush on her."

"But she only has eyes for the Universe (praise be unto Him)."

"I know. The Commander's love seems silly-false."

"How true," muses Biendoror with a slight smile, "And also how highly inconvenient to us. I imagine our presence is requested yet again?"

Jixim confirms by reciting, "A certain number of those who are not dubious and so forth are requested to witness the ordeal."

"This Commander is out of control."

"So are you coming with me, then?"

"Sure."

II

In mid-town, Jixim and Biendoror arrive at the very end of Central Thoroughfare, where the street proper leads to the conveyor belt that carries the dubious testees to their test. The audience is arrayed in stands on either side of the conveyor's path, but many prefer to stand.

"What do you think of the fashions this season?" asks Jixim, as he surveys the crowd.

"Ha. Normally I don't consider them. But the latest offerings are quite severe. Almost anxious," answers Biendoror.

"There's a rush in the atmosphere. Of course it would find its way into the hemlines and collar sizes."

"I defer to your stance in such matters. But I am feeling the associations you report."

"If they think I'm going to surrender my floor-length black leather jacket in favor of the gilded breastplate . . ."

"Yeah?"

"Well, I may just oblige them."

"With or without heraldry medallions?"

"With. Without accoutrements, I'm nude."

A man with double hair arches walks past. Biendoror smirks. "What about those arches? Aren't they supposed to allude to regality?"

"No, only to the fact that regality is on your mind. That the two halves of you are in harmony with the reign."

"Well, it seems to me that if more citizens *achieved* that harmony, there'd be less need for these testing rituals."

"Assuming, of course, that the Police Commander is not himself a prize dunderhead."

Biendoror sighs. "Lord help his ass. He is a scourge scoundrel without restraint."

"I want him to be tested," Jixim declares.

Biendoror nods and says, with muted though palpable glee, "In at least one likely tomorrow, he is tribulated."

A fanfare calls out on a platinum horn blown by a police bugler.

"Look, even the police bugler's uniform is less traditional."

One by one, nervous testees begin walking onto the conveyor. They ride it for about a block, and step off at the end, one at a time, onto an ejector which then hurls them into the Energy Wall of the Heart. Those who can pass go right through the energy mass and land snugly on the other side, feeling great calm and power. They are verified. Others smash into the Energy Wall, as it is solid and unyielding to them. They are momentarily flattened against it . . . or at least it appears that way. Their noses turn a bright magenta red and stay that way for about six or seven days. They are now called the *unpassed.*

After the first few tests, a police captain shakes his head and says, as though it were a grand discovery, "Some pass, and some do not."

"Hmm," says Jixim, "A fair amount of pretenders today. May they not be fast on their way to being slaves."

"They better do their homework. Oh, but they will," states Biendoror, half-aloud and half to himself.

"Or they'll be doing my housework," Jixim responds. "They'll do what's proper, I'm sure. Or maybe not. I really don't care. Sometimes I think it's easier to decide such things when there's no choice at all."

Biendoror nods, adding, "The best is not even choosing to not choose."

"Wait, let's hear what the Judger says to the un-passed."

The Judger—a portly man with a languid air—sits down calmly in his massive official chair and surveys the crowd with a couple glances. "Heaveno, everyone. There is no judgment from me because the Wall has already done that." The Judger, so-called, gets up and leaves.

"That which is good and brief is good twice over," states Jixim.

"Indeed," smiles Biendoror.

"In deed as well as in fact," smirks an older gentle-man.

"In fact as it is in act," offers Jixim.

The old gent frowns anxiously and walks off brisk-ly, occasionally looking back with a worried expres-sion.

About half the crowd stays put, sensing more pro-cedures may be announced, but the rest—including Jixim and Biendoror—take the Judger at his word and begin breaking off. Our friends decide to stroll about town.

"Did you notice how, instead of his customary long brown robes, the Judger wore a miniskirt?" Jixim asks Biendoror as they walk.

"Yes, and I think it went rather nicely with the tease of a performance he gave."

"Why have him there at all? Eventually, he'll be wearing nothing but a pasty," speculates Jixim.

Biendoror nods. "Oh, he'll feel overdressed even then. Officials have little flair for fashion, beauty, or sense. Even I know that."

"Hmm. My dear Biendoror, clothes reflect the spirit of the life force as it takes form at any given juncture. What incoherence, then, for officials to be finely arrayed."

"Thank you for confirming that clothes are more than a cover."

Suddenly a woman dressed in sensible linens that hold no decor shouts at both our friends, "My, gents, but how frivolous we are today! See here, louts, do you not work for a living even while others work themselves to dying?"

Jixim and Biendoror instantly note that she is older by the elegant lines etched on her face. They also admire the utilized grace of her artisans' hands and the hinted-at delicacy of the collarbones pushing up her taught skin. Nevertheless, despite all this beauty, she is quite upset.

Biendoror is amused. "What is this, Jixim, a one-woman Slave's Rebellion?"

"Throw clay today, woman?" Jixim asks with that aplomb which is uniquely his.

The woman stands there, stunned, mouth slightly agape.

"Now you see here, woman. I just openly acknowledged your status as a slave, which I would never do unless you were declaring your liberty, so which shall it be?"

The woman stands there, more stunned, mouth more than slightly agape. She teeters a little bit, and then confesses, "I'm dreaming. I know exactly how to go about living now."

"Well, if that's the case, then thrice-welcome!" offers Jixim.

"Indeed, by the holy heart of the Eagle, come well," affirms Biendoror.

"Giving thanks to you both," she returns.

"Tell me, lady, what is your old name?" ventures Jixim.

"Magnotta," she answers.

"And your new name?"

"Magmana."

"Well done, very apt," Biendoror determines. "You

are clearly a fightrix."

"And I declare you're the type who gives quarter," adds Jixim.

She blushes lightly, the sign of still-new freedom.

"I hope you do something with those magnificent lines on your face," asserts Jixim. "I would paint them different colors, make them stand out."

"That could be your warpaint," Biendoror adds.

Magmana smiles. "I think I'll don a new satin and snakeskin cowl with a toga of swastikas and hexa-grams."

"Fine, off with you then," winks Jixim.

"Pasties are only an apparent option," Biendoror offers enigmatically.

"Great bye," concludes Magmana.

Jixim and Biendoror walk off. "She has a refreshing effect," opines Biendoror.

"She reminds me of someone," Jixim replies.

"Requesting your pardon, gentlemen . . ." An agent of the Police Commandery, identified by his scarlet uniform and floppy knitted cap, addresses them as he walks closer. ". . . but the Commander requests your presence at the tribulation being held shortly, for the benefit of today's unpassed."

Jixim and Biendoror look at one another.

Biendoror: "How shortly?"

"At N hours," the agent responds.

Jixim emits consternation. "Why us? We just come from witnessing the test."

"I know, I remember you. That is why. I'm signaling all today's witnesses. The Commander has decided to speed up and unite the process. You'll be among the same crowd as earlier."

III

"Look at them out there," says a voice from the shadows of a roofed alley, "so joyous in their well-earned freeness."

His companion silently watches the people walking about. "Do they love being free?"

"I don't know or care," responds the first shadowy figure. "What scalds me is they distinguish between free and slave, high and low, clean and dirty. How nice of them to do, being already on the other side! But I'm changing all that, from the inside out. For every single one will be on the same level. The day of masters and servants is almost done."

"Our plan was set in rotation," his companion reflects. "But what of this way of Succession for the new Empress, spawned by Vatvoy? It came so soon and unexpected, and prevents Discontinuity."

"It doesn't matter. We'll kill her too." He smiles at his companion. "Would you like her to be dead?"

"Oh, yes," the companion answers slowly. "It has to be. No one is going to lord it over me again."

IV

Biendoror and Jixim are at Tribulation Grounds, their irked mood soothed somewhat by the openness of the space and its cool dusky ambience. The spectacle begins quietly. The unpassed walk up barefoot in a single file, wearing only pink smocks and pink skullcaps with red bull horns. Iron poles are arrayed at intervals around the perimeter of a vast oval pool filled with clear water (the Fool Pool). Each unpassed gets led to a pole, and is tied to it. An agent goes around, asking each in turn to bite into a golden green apple and hold it with his or her teeth.

The hushed crowd watches standing, but the two dozen highest officers of the Commandery watch sitting in their gazebo. Sitting in the middle of the front row is the Commander himself, and just behind him sits his assistant, the Top Secretary of the Police Commandery.

Acting as ceremony master, the Top Secretary rises and announces, "This is your chance to keep yourself from descending into slavery!" Each unpassed understands this is directed to him or her personally.

The Archer, wearing a transparent hood with two eye holes, comes out from behind the gazebo with his crossbow and quiver of golden arrows. He steps onto a little boat at the water's edge, grabs hold of a long oar and, standing in the middle of the boat, silently makes his way to the center of the Fool Pool. Once there, he calmly places an arrow in his bow, draws, aims it at an unpassed's mouth, and lets it go. The apple is instantly pierced, but still held by the servant's mouth. The servant looks rather shaken, but is doing well. The crowd remains quiet and still. The Archer places another arrow in his bow, aims it at another unpassed's mouth, and shoots. Again, an apple is pierced. The Archer repeats this procedure for each of the unpassed, one by one. Unusually, not a single one gets hurt or killed. Done, he holds his crossbow high with his right hand. The Top Secretary stands and announces, "The sign of the Crossbow!" The Archer rows back to the edge of the pool, steps off the boat, walks toward the gazebo, and disappears behind it.

They are untied and free to go, ending their only opportunity for tribulation. "This batch must've learned their lesson of living," Biendoror whispers.

V

Our two protagonists sit in a downtown liquids & aethers shop, sipping fungoo brew and talking politics.

Jixim leans back comfortably in his cushion chair. "I hope the Commander eases up. These tests and things are more and more common now of days. And my vow is on us getting summoned for witnessing yet again."

"It seems he's an eager ogre to prevent the dubious people from becoming slaves," Biendoror muses.

"Sure, sure. But it's their power to lose."

Biendoror ponders this, then . . . "The tests catch the problem. And the tribulations teach those unpassed the slave path's folly so they may keep mastering themselves. There's no other way to go about it. The Empire flowers with more free people, not less." He pauses a moment and sighs, "But witnessing is indeed a chore."

"So you can force freedom on the people?" Jixim wonders.

"No, but if someone is slipping, they deserve that chance to be tribulated and decide clearly. That is, if they survive the tribulation."

Jixim shrugs.

"Hey, should we inhale some chocolate?" asks Biendoror.

"We should," replies Jixim, showing renewed vim. "Waitrix, two chookahs."

She smiles and takes a few steps closer to their table. "With tincture?"

Jixim notices Biendoror's pleasure at the suggestion, and looks at the waitrix. "Both with."

The waitrix nods but her attention is on Jixim's uniform. "Right away." Her eyes flit from his epaulets to his sash to his peaked cap. She pauses. "I . . . see by your regalia that you're a Forcefield Marshall of the A.E.I.O.U. [Alchemical Echelons In Omni-Universality]."

"That's true. My compliments on your knowledge of such a recondite matter."

She smiles brilliantly and it can't but be noticed. And her burgundy lips perfectly match her eyes and hair.

Jixim asks, "Say, how is it that one so young can decipher the insignia on an A.E.I.O.U. uniform?"

Reading his meaning, she says, "I'm not a servant as such. I run this shop since I have deep love for it, but same-wise I aspire to contribute more freely and subtly, and have made the various Orders of the Empire my objects of passion."

Biendoror interjects, "So you prepare for initiation into one of the Forces?"

"Not yet. I'm not sure which one I'm suited for."

"That's fine," asserts Jixim. "They'll suit you and dress you up once you're admitted. Your uniform and ensembles will then gradually reveal who you are—so far as duty goes—as you wear them."

"Just make sure you never become an official," suggests Biendoror.

"An official?"

"Yes, any member of an Order who just takes up space, who clogs things up. Or any bureaucrat."

Jixim says slyly, "As far as I'm concerned, they're fast on their way to being servants."

"I don't know why the Empire uses them," wonders Biendoror.

"Because it is much too generous," Jixim suggests.

"Thanks for these teachings," the waitrix says warmly. Remembering herself suddenly: "Oh, I better get your chookahs." She walks off and looks back with an almost-wink. "My name is Ralama."

They both look on as she goes to the back of the shop. "Did you hear that, Jixim? She may go quite far."

Jixim stares quietly. "Yes, the name is masterful."

Another voice speaks. "The keys to a name, the sheer alchemy of its sonic and historic components, are simply beyond the purview of a slave. They rarely, if ever, choose propitiously." A middle-aged gentleman sitting at a nearby table. "You hear how she clarified that she's free? She runs this place. Doesn't merely work here. It's cute. But, you see, many of our young today play with these servant-like roles . . . until they confirm within who they really are. Before that, they may not want to wear the marks of the free."

"Good points, one and all," responds Biendoror. "Do you think it has to do with the Change in Succession?"

The gentleman's expression briefly hints he hadn't considered this. "I don't know. It may. Anything that Vatvoy touches is bound to be odd," he laughs.

"Even if it's a whole aeon," agrees Jixim.

VI

In the heart of Central Thoroughfare, within the headquarters citadel of the Free Force (F.F.), the great parent Order, Jixim and Biendoror get briefed by a lead officer named Dulcon in a conferring room overlooking the city from on high. Called clairaudiently while walking nearby, they now sit back in sapphire-silver chairs while Dulcon stands before them.

"Gents, in regard of your talents, you've been summoned for this report to help the F.F. in a question most unexpected."

"I, for one, feel glad helping," Biendoror shares.

"As I do," echoes Jixim.

"Giving warmth," Dulcon responds. "The issue at hand is the imminent return of the Cat. The signs we perceive indicate he plans to use communication magic to cause the people—all of them—to equate slavery with freedom."

"Do you mean the Bat?" asks Biendoror.

"No," answers Dulcon, "we get nothing of his." With easy calm, he rests his back against the marble wall behind him.

"So," Jixim clarifies, "this Cat means to blur the divides between servants and free people by making them sound the same?"

"Yes. Or even by making slavery seem better."

"Tell us more about the Cat," requests Biendoror. "His name hasn't been spoken in so long. Has he changed?"

"Nothing we get is certain," answers Dulcon. "But some say his apparel looks different. He now wears blue and red and has renounced purple and green."

"All these changes give me the horrors," Jixim states plainly. His eyes brighten. "On the other hand, they help me tingle with thrills."

Dulcon nods lightly. "The Cat's specialty was, notoriously, to interrupt tribulations. In olden days, he would arrive suddenly, mock the proceedings, and crown his intervention by leaving his mark of amber elixir on or near the gazebo."

"Naturally, the Commandery loathed this," Jixim observes.

"*Most* naturally," retorts Dulcon. "It ruined the lesson in the one and only ritual those unpassed could have."

Biendoror feels absorbed while viewing the old past in his head. He smiles from cheek to cheek. "And he wasn't ever stopped, was he?"

"He got caught once but then escaped. The Commandery couldn't hold, let alone change, him. No matter what they did to him, he'd stay the same and be mysteriously happy and serene. Unique slave, to not be intimidated! You know the Commandery can be rough. One day, he confused his captors and disappeared from them." Dulcon rubs his chin. "Impressed by all this, some agents felt moved to even doubt slavery's inferiority. . . ."

"And others to doubt the Cat was truly a slave," Biendoror adds. "Some speculated he was really a renegade free person."

"A slavelover," Jixim comments.

"Yes," agrees Dulcon cautiously, "but the notion of slaveloving was called too perverse by the old Emperor. It was one of the few things he ever said. The Commandery bowed to him. Slaveloving seemed incredible. . . . But today we know the Cat is a master who doesn't understand slavery."

"But his self-mastery isn't absolute?" Jixim asks.

"We don't think so, but it packs heft. His feats tell us that much. He sheds the rays of strength. Anyway, absolute mastery is such a rare bird." Dulcon looks out the office's panoramic crystal window as the Pelican flies by, no doubt wholly absorbed in making his rounds. He turns back to his two guests. "The Cat's origins are as unknown as a slave's. Who he is and where he comes from, no one can say. The problem is we *want* to know. The archives are silent. But he embodies a further mystery: that a free person can work hard for slavery's glory and remain free, and even impress. To not lose your power promoting ignorance is miraculous."

"So what now?" checks Biendoror.

"His chosen exile done, the Cat is setting to work right away. Like a slave, he values time and doesn't waste it. It is said he has taken up with the Scorpion. We're not sure when this happened, or whether it was he who sent the Scorpion to kill the Emperor."

Jixim and Biendoror turn to read one another and then back to Dulcon.

He fiddles absently with the yellow medal on his grey tunic. "Gents, he means to strike the people with true falsehoods. Oh, he is clever. Mark it well. The tricks that a master can play on a slave, the Cat plays with free people! He may be a master's master, and is a menace. He *begs* for being dealt with. So we summon you to duty. We want to try something in a new vein, and need unconventional blood he's never faced."

"Ah, in that case," says Jixim, "I have just the right person in heart and mind."

VII

Hereta lurks in a lonely sector—one favored by servants and criminal slavemongers. She wears her new platform flight boots, which allow her to leap and fly about, as willed by her purposeful muscle twitches. At one moment, she is on the ledge of a high tower; at another, hovering under a bridge; at yet another, looking down on passing tenements and forgotten alleyways.

She thinks, "I'm deputized by Jixim to covertly patrol this sector due to a rumor that the Cat is planning a comeback, possibly in cahoots with the

Scorpion. Jixim's new thoughts are that, unlike the Scorpion, the Cat should be stopped in his paw tracks. But with regard to the other, Jixim's soul knows that only the Scorpion can—and eventually will—defeat himself." As she courses through the air and feels a warm flow inside, Hereta smiles invisibly at how hot burns her ardor to work her skills and go past her apprenticeship. Indeed, her new boots are filled nicely.

Her eyes narrow into two squint slits as she catches sight of a still figure below; somehow a familiar form, though she knows she's never seen it; sure no free person has, other than the old Emperor in his last days. Sensing it feels weak, she lands near it.

"Could it be that I find him like this, so easily? The Scorpion! Wait. No, it's not him." She counts his ten legs and recalls her recent training. "This is the Lobster, mightiest counterpart and most hated rival of the Scorpion. Found lying mortally injured among a heap of boxes, riddled with holes."

"That's right," the Lobster barely affirms, his two enormous claws snipping aimlessly at the air. "After all these years, he finally got me. And all because of my forbidden choice to abandon the formula SLAVERY > FREEDOM. As long as we were slave foes, no need to kill."

"You want to be free?"

"Yes, and now I am."

"There is no time but the present. Welcome to wisdom."

He nods.

"Can you tell me, my love, what are his plans and do they involve the Cat?" Hereta inquires.

"I don't know, child. But I believe he's the strongest holdout against freedom. Is proud of slavery, and, and . . . wants to enslave the free people."

Hereta opens wide her eyes, impressed at the grotesque grandeur of the ambition.

The Lobster notes her response and smiles. "His tail is, in effect, his brain."

She touches his hard skin.

He says, "I thank you."

She presses on him warmly and he passes through.

VIII

Jixim, Biendoror, and Hereta meet at the F.F. citadel with Dulcon's partner Dulcama. She wears a gray uniform with a silver ruffle collar, and white and blue medals over her right and left nipples, respectively. Hereta wears a thin, almost sheer, white lambskin toga with an alexandrite brooch, and is barefoot. She speaks out first.

"My encounter with the Lobster, now deceased, on my mission through one of the nearer Slaville sectors tells me there's a rift within the slave realm. More servants are realizing they're enslaved. Ordinarily, that's good. But instead of going for freedom, some linger in slavery and then make a cult of it. These want to stop the others from going free."

Dulcama purses her lips and smacks them softly. Her expression is earnest. "Perhaps they're afraid of making that leap over the abyss. And they can't deal with the shame."

Biendoror interjects, "This is extraordinary. Slaves who know they are, and choose to remain, slaves!"

"It doesn't begin to make sense . . . which is doubtless the point," Jixim says coolly as he studies his buffed fingernails.

"It aims to negate love, life and liberty," opines Dulcama. "Hereta, who did the Lobster in?"

"The Scorpion," Hereta replies. "With no sign of the Cat." She pauses. "The Lobster died free."

"He would have made a fine ally," Dulcama judges. "But we should be clear that not every slave who wakes up blossoms into real freedom. The Scorpion, of course, being the prime example. This type of slave is much more formidable and is bound to cause trouble. He is less rare these days. What separates him from the typical servant is that, instead of not knowing about freedom, he hates it."

Jixim shakes his head. "Such a ruffian doesn't love both the . . ."

Suddenly, the desktop news head makes an announcement. "A special tribulation is being held today at R hours, you know where. The Police Commander has invited her absolute altitude, the Empress, as guest of honor, and she has harmoniously accepted. Exquisiteness is in the air!"

The news head stops.

"Did you hear that, Biendoror?" Jixim asks. "The Commander is in love."

Hereta and Dulcama are quiet.

Biendoror makes a pensive face. "This is without precedent. A Commander inviting an Empress to a tribulation. Where will she sit?"

"I'm sure he's plotting to be her throne," Jixim speculates.

Hereta and Dulcama giggle.

"And yet . . ." says Biendoror.

"Yes, you're right!" Jixim exclaims.

"Oh, of course," reflects Dulcama. "But do you think the trap is too obvious?"

"It's not a trap," Hereta states. "I sense the Commander is acting from his heart."

"Maybe so," responds Biendoror. "But the Cat will likely grab the chance to ruin this special tribulation. And, with the Empress there, the Commander will have heavy guards. Waiting. Ready to pounce on this Cat."

"I agree," Dulcama sighs. "But the Cat may yet bowl them all over. His powers are strange. As you know, he's done it before."

"We should go too," offers Jixim. "It could get hot, and I don't want to risk the Empress."

"Remember, though," says Biendoror with a far-seeing look in his eyes, "it's going to be an afternoon of great love and great hate."

IX

At the special tribulation, everyone is dressed to the nines in their best *rituel* outfits. The Empress sits in the Commander's seat wearing a matching dress and mask made entirely of orchids, lilies and sunflowers, stitched just so with silk vines; while the Commander sits at her feet, having capped his usual uniform with the tall maroon fur helmet that is the Commander's right to wear on occasions of honor. While everyone is busy hoping to outshine everyone else, the surprise of the day is the usually-demure Biendoror in his black-and-white cowhide ensemble with pointed tawny leather boots, what with their massive gold and pyrite buckles that seem to reach out and tease you on at least three different levels. And, ringing the pool, flanks of crimson-bedecked agents smartly holding up the numerous esoteric standards of the Commandery's divisions and companies, fluttering here and there as the cool breeze blows. Meanwhile, the sun shines grandly upon this matinée tribulation.

Several guards keep the unpassed herded away to the side, and look frequently toward the gazebo for the signal to conduct their charges toward the pool's perimeter. But the Top Secretary pleasantly walks to the front of the gazebo and addresses the crowd. "Gents and ladies of the Realm, I want to grant . . ."

"Oooooo! Eeeeeooooo!" "Ooooooooh! Eeeeeeeeee-oooooooooh!" "Ooooeeeeeeeeooooooooooooooooh!" The plaintive, yet deeply mocking, yelp fills the scene.

"Brace yourself," says Jixim to his group. "It's getting interesting."

"Sacred shit, it's the Cat!" shouts one onlooker.

"Where?" responds another.

"I think I see, or just saw, him."

A nearby audience member points excitedly. "He's here. He's there. No, he's here. Yes, he's not here."

The Cat tantalizes the attendees, allowing them a

peek of him here and there, but then clouds their minds at will—just enough so they don't notice him even as he stands right in front of them. And then he lets them spot him again, but he's in a different place now, so that by the sudden contrast in location they realize he's toying with them. His presence is inside their heads, as well as out, and he lets them feel it. Seemingly, he masters them with ease, leaping—or is it materializing?—anywhere he pleases at any time. No one considers making a move against him: even the Commandery guards stay still.

The crowd is rife with shouted speculation.

"Look! He looks deadlier than he used to!"

"Is he a secret agent for one of the Orders?"

"Thanking heaven he's come! What always made these ceremonies back then was these glorious, crashing interruptions."

The Cat regally approaches the area in front of the gazebo to address the crowd and show off, to best effect, his elegantly simple jumpsuit of black fur with navy blue and plum red velvet. He speaks smilingly. "A special tribulation, indeed. For how often is the Commander himself tribulated?"

The crowd gasps at this audacity, in no small part because it feels convincing.

A couple of slaves appear from behind the gazebo

and apprehend the stunned Commander, taking him to one of the poles lining the pool and securing him to it, hands tied behind his back. His mouth is offered an apple and accepts it.

The crowd is riveted, either unable or unwilling to move.

Seemingly out of nowhere, the Cat produces the crossbow, already loaded with a golden arrow. He takes aim with it, and scoffs, "Everyone knows officers of the Commandery aren't real police . . . they're commers! Now, officers of the Temple . . . those are true police knights." He shoots, and a loud cracking sound is heard from the Commander's mouth as his head goes limp. "There. So much for the lover. Next time, don't set a test you won't pass." He slowly scans the crowd and settles on the gazebo, homing in on the Empress. "Now here's the little lady lord."

The two slave drones delicately carry her from the gazebo to the edge of the pool, each holding her there by one arm, insecurely, due to the pure royal energy she gives off.

With a sweep of his hand, the Cat announces, "And now, friends . . . I present you my good companion, the imperocidal Scorpion!"

As the crowd gasps loudly, the Scorpion sticks his head out from behind the gazebo, followed by his whole body. He makes his way to the Empress with his stinger looming forward suggestively, even lewdly.

The Cat looks on, pleased and proud. "With this act—the Empress dying by sting and the Empire no longer having a head—I will make all free people slaves. But not myself a slave am. That is my supreme sacrifice to make. Instead of delighting in simple rest and strife, my destiny is to run things. Oh, the worry!" Said with a leering wink.

Jixim makes an effort to look over at Biendoror, but it's very difficult. It's as though his desire to not see overtakes his will to look. He thinks he senses Biendoror still sitting by his side. He also suspects Hereta and Dulcama remain on his other side, but isn't sure. The simplest things feel doubtful.

The Cat continues. "Slavery is the high point of all life, for not knowing you're really *alive,* you have no power over yourself or the cares that come with power. And if you have rudely awakened into freedom, how nice to get back to sleep!"

The Cat turns and looks up at the sky, amber eyes seething with glee. "Someone said I look deadlier than before. Yes, I am deadlier. Far from losing my force by pushing slavery, I gain *more.* That's a secret the free people don't know, even as I reveal it."

"Fool! Every free person knows that, they're just

not low enough to accede to it!" The Police Commander. In one hand he holds the green apple with the golden arrow sticking through, and hurls it point-first deftly right into the Cat's heart, saying, "You speak very much."

The Cat's eyes are wide open. "How?"

"You got in my head, but not my gut. And my gut said to make a false noise and play dead. Isn't it something how I pass?"

The Cat collapses to the ground like a bag of rags, clutching his forehead with one paw and his breast with the other, as he dies. The Scorpion slides into the pool, makes his way to the bottom, and disappears by opening one of the gratings.

Feline spell broken, the crowd loosens up and moves about more freely, with shouts of relief and offers of compassion dominating. The guards and high officers attend to the Empress and Commander, who are slightly shaken but fine. The Cat's slaves are seized.

Jixim turns to his companions. "I may have judged the Commander too harshly. He definitely impresses. I don't know how he did it." Hereta rubs Jixim's shoulder, pleased at his reconsideration.

Biendoror grins sheepishly. Jixim fixes a still gaze on him. Biendoror hesitates and then admits, "Well, it helps a mite that I delayed the Cat's perception eight seconds, from the time he had the Empress brought out. And I do mean *time*." Biendoror laughs. "What the Cat then saw happening really happened eight seconds earlier. So he was behind everyone else and couldn't catch up, and didn't even know he had to. Which is good because the Commander, while clever, isn't the fastest chap around. Anyway, time is a sort of opinion about movement, and it can be molded. . . ." Biendoror notices that no one—not even Jixim—shows any interest in his technique. He sighs, "Sorry. It has to do with my own special science."

Hereta hugs him. "And that's why we adore you, B."

"Well," says Jixim, "I'm still pleased the Commander pulled it off, though his politics irk me. And by 'politics' I mean 'making me come to Commandery rituals.' Something tells me the drive for them is cooling. But, for the next one, I'll be ready. You won't believe what I'm going to wear. Sorry, chum, but it'll make this outfit of yours look like a folded sandpaper hat."

While Jixim generally doesn't like politics, on principle he loves it anyway as his own duty. He engages it with love, making love to it until he loves it. "That's the power of love," says Jixim.

"THE SQUIRREL IN THE SKY"

I

It's a beauteous day, with the sun, moons and the seven local planets shining forth together across the city's terrain in nacreous numinosity. It follows that a groundswell of calm joy occupies the people.

Jixim and Hereta drink in and sniff up the sights while they walk the streets of the Neighborhood Shopping Disco. Jixim—as is his wont since being taught by Biendoror—periodically notes the occasional supernova, and keeps track of the sunspot cycles, with his mental observatory. This seemingly irks Hereta to no end.

"You're doing it again. You promised you'd slow down today."

Jixim leaves aside his astral games and spots the various wares on display in their cylindrical crystal holders. "At least I'm not morphing products."

"Oh, but I wish you would. You have me figured out all wrong. In fact . . . could you change those peek-a-boo gloves into a plumed fedora? If you can, I'll take them."

"No, that's too distracting."

"You can do it at home . . . later."

"You're as sweet as you are impertinent," he smiles, picking up the gloves while vaguely admiring them with a furtive half-twinkle in one of his eyes. "Do you realize how the exposed fingertips make these useless for crime? Wearing them is tantamount to declaring one's allegiance to all that is Law. Agents of the Police Temple should wear at least one."

"But then criminals might wear them as a ruse," observes Hereta.

"It's the power of the symbol, my dear toots. Wearing them may heighten their latent reluctance."

A band walks onto the showcase and begins playing on four synesthesizers. The music is as horrific as it is ecstatic.

Many of the people begin to smile, dance and whirl.

"Hmm. Touching," Jixim notes. "The Devil's Scale in counterpoint to the Divine Octave. Brilliant. Impish, in fact. Reminding us that Chaos is Order misperceiv'd. Taunting us with it, adoring us."

"Chaorder?" asks Hereta.

"How could we ever forget?" Jixim ponders with some wonder.

One of the synesthesizerists emits a solo in spiraling pink lasers.

"This song is scrumptious, yet bitter," a nearby dancer declares.

A young satisfied beauty asserts, "This is the best chunk of music I've caressed in a while."

One guy standing next to her agreeably huffs, "You could noticeably age a slab of granite in the time since I last felt something so fully."

Our featured couple walks on, and as the music recedes ever more into the background, Hereta says, "Oh Jixim, I'm so happy that these scamps value the song's force!"

Jixim mimes the musicians' poses on the stage, and with a sneer says, "And it goes like *this!* Fuck all about, people!"

Hereta giggles and freely laughs out loud, with a tear moving down her cheek. With her approval, everything is making her very happy, especially seeing the latest goods offered, such as the backpack ornithopters *("Fly like the Vulture!"),* and, even more, sensing how the people enjoy the time.

About to break into a cossack dance, Jixim begins swiveling his hips back and forth, and notes, "Look how the sunlight touches my arm. It almost looks like it's disappearing instead of bouncing off!"

Hereta nods before a loud drone is heard, a drone quite unlike any other. It oddly feels like it has mass and yet is also a void. The people still walk about in joy but slower than before, and gradually still themselves with uncertainty and curiosity as the sound becomes more conspicuous. After a few moments, the sound is the object of everyone's attention.

"Jixim, what . . . ?" Hereta begins.

"Shh," says Jixim.

The sound becomes more distinct, and now drones like a growl-scream. It appears to be coming from very far away, yet also from right next to every one of the people. On the horizon lies a thing, a sort of manimal made entirely of glowing multicolored rings and cones. Yet, though they glow, they shed no light. The thing appears to be many miles in size, and the sky's hue changes almost constantly in response to its presence, as if trying to expel it.

Biendoror appears by Jixim and Hereta's sides. "What is it, that thing?"

"I don't know. It's about as big as the sky wall," Jixim answers. "May the Eagle peck it."

The people now generally stand still, saying little, rapt in awe at the disturbing enormity.

"Look at those colors, something's wrong with them," observes Jixim.

Biendoror narrows his gaze. Then he smiles, though seriously. "Those aren't colors so much as analogs of colors. This creature is made of pitch darkness but is somehow suggesting these imitations of light."

"Charming."

The droning wail-howl breaks up into discrete rhythms like the on-and-off blowing of a metallic bass wind, and these become words that are wholly unknown. But their meaning gets decoded, more or less, as they reach the ear.

"Kashimaná modjo! Chickle chanks chickle chanks! Poto susio hiel! Flinz! Chonqaster!"

"What's it saying?" asks Hereta, as she realizes the answer. More thunderous word screeches continue.

"These Billy Kids today, with their crazy speak," Jixim says grinning, as he notices Hereta's realization.

"Well, I be," remarks Biendoror, "It issues its pronouncements. Makes its presence known from the horizon. It wants the monetary value of all our world's things—objects, people, land, ideas, and more. Or it will take the things themselves, even though they're worthless to him."

"Monetary. . . . What says Biendoror, my lifelong palomino? Bluff or tough?" Jixim curiously asks.

"Enough huff," replies Biendoror thoughtfully. "It's 'time' for us to go." They slip away to another place, with him guiding.

II

In the center of the Police Temple, various agents and officers present their reports on the Monster to the High Police Priest, who has control authority over all police matters. Taking notes by his side is his assistant, the Police Commander. The central chamber of the Temple is ample and nicely lit by electronic fluid torches. Down the middle of the vast room, the long conferring table is crowded due to the urgency of the crisis.

The High Police Priest feels flustered. He now has much information but no *knowledge*. "So the Monster is very, very big. And he's mean, he's made of false light, he has ascended from another plane, and is perfectly still and composed so that he may never be dislodged. And, lest we all forget, he produces loud annoying noise. Personally, I'm not convinced he's alive. That has not yet been determined."

The congregation of high-ranking Law personnel, or Police Council, looks on expectantly.

The High Police Priest continues. "But . . . what does he want? What does he want? If we know that, we have the key. Even if we can't find the lock, having the key is so nice! Do all agree?!"

"Yes, sire!" bellows the congregation.

"But what does he want?" the High Priest of Police asks emptily.

"Money." A short, bookish officer stands at the door and walks up to the great table to take a seat. "Sire, Agent Tamo, Knowledge Division and Multiplication." He sits and joins the other officers. "What the Monster wants is money. If he gets it, he won't take our world."

"What is money?" inquires the High Police Priest.

"Very difficult to explain," replies Agent Tamo. "It's an arithmetical or quantitative symbol that in other planes is used to acquire things."

"Acquire things? Like with a series of mechanical claws?"

"No, no. In trade. You trade an amount of the symbol for whatever things you want whose agreed worth equates to that precise amount of the symbol."

"A form of barter."

"Yes."

"Only even more stupid."

"Certainly."

"So then, Agent Tamo? . . . you can't—in these planes—simply have things because it's right to, or because you deserve them, or because you want them. In addition, you need to have this money symbol."

"Right."

"Ah," the High Priest wonders, "so does everyone have all the money they need?"

"Not at all, certainly. It's a peculiarity of money that, when there's too much of it, it's worth less. So there has to be more demanding than supply. That doesn't hold if everyone has an optimum amount. And with money not worth anything, there's no point to it."

"But with this demanding arrangement, many people in these planes likely spend their lives distracted chasing this money, and fretting over it."

"That is apparently what happens there. For it to work, the few handle supply while the many engage in demanding. People of both groups battle to own more of the symbol. In fact, aside from any incidental nobleness and well-being due to creating and sharing things, it shapes their world with an interminable series of death blows. Or, at least, knockout punchouts."

The High Police Priest peers at the officer with aroused interest. "Tell me more, Tamo. So we can plot a scheme."

"I have no more, sire. That is all the secret archives say. And I have no contact experience with the meaner planes."

One of the councilors stands and asks impulsively,

"Should we consult the Empress?"

A nearby councilor stands and opposes the motion: "The Empress is ruling us and being who she is. She is not a problem-solver!"

The High Police Priest smirks and looks down thoughtfully. "Who has experience visiting an accursed plane?"

"Vatvoy, sire," a chief agent replies.

"Hmm. Who else?"

"Santrisen, an excellent planar navigator and researcher at the Multiversity."

"Bring him to me!"

The chief agent makes a mudra with his left hand and says, "Sire, he's on his way. . . ."

III

Jixim, Hereta and Biendoror are in Biendoror's living room, sharing a bottle of grapefruit-and-eggplant wine. The pressing strains of the Monster's utterances barely make their way, muffled and slight, through the walls of his townhouse.

"These walls have an inner lining of gold, which his frequencies respect," offers Biendoror by way of explanation. "Lots of walls are lined with silver or copper, which are less effective."

"Aren't slaves' walls usually lined with iron?" Hereta questions.

"Yes. Otherwise they strip the walls of their linings. Seems the splendor guides their hearts," Biendoror responds.

"They do so many things oppositely to us," Jixim notes.

"They're not in touch with their good gut god so much," muses Biendoror.

"But what's beautiful is you can see the power of their potential just laying there," Hereta states.

Biendoror opens his eyes wider. "Speaking of power potential, I think this may be time to work out my idea for an electromagnetic quantum guitar."

"And you plan to point the singer cabinet toward the Monster to serenade it?" chuckles Jixim.

"I want to. Feel this out: the lute is to have eleven main strings, but each one has a corresponding course of eleven resonating strings tuned to an ingeniously microtonal scale that not only exalts reason but completely baffles it. There are thus 132 strings in total, but it is truly one long string periodically stopped by numerous capos. Not only that, but the string, body, bridge, tuners, and all the components are made of differently shaped sections of one continuous slab of aureous platinum. The whole lute is absolutely of a piece, resonating in its beauty unity."

"Heaveno, it tastes like one inferno of a loot! Let's work it out now," Jixim says with passion.

"Yes, let's," concurs Biendoror.

"This is turning into boys' work," says Hereta with a lop-sided smile, as she stands up.

"Are you going?" asks Jixim.

"Yes," she answers, clasping the back of his neck and kissing the corner of his mouth.

IV

The one they call Santrisen arrives at the entrance to the Police Council Chamber. He wears a green cowl, lime pantaloons, and red cottonball slippers. His face is centered by a little square white mustache. He quietly bows to the High Police Priest, who looks him over in an instant and answers with a nod.

"Your name is Santrisen?"

"Yes, sire."

"You are acquainted with money and the worlds that deal in it?"

"Yes, sire. With some of them."

"Summarize your knowledge in one comment."

"Things there aren't free for the taking . . . or the giving."

"How can anyone have freedom if nothing is free?"

"The key is that only nothing is free."

"How do you propose we overturn this Moneyster or Monster?"

"Overturn, sire?"

"Destabilize it, fluster it. Help it lose its grip. That way, we can destructure it with greater ease. You should know he is perfectly cold. Unrelenting in his focus. Void of any apparent feeling or irrationality."

"So we should vex him somehow?"

"Quite rightly. Introduce him to decontrol, even if it's just an inkling. Maybe have him feel love. A successful method is greatly preferred. You are up to it?"

"Sire, if you want to overturn the Monster, I suggest you give it everything it wants."

"The Empire should appease it? I anticipate a most exalted scandal!"

"That's not it, sire. You see, the secret of money in the prison planes is that it doesn't really exist. Other than as an idea for the people to believe in and then conduct themselves accordingly. So giving this Monster all the money in the universe is as difficult as spitting or smiling."

The councilors and agents murmur among themselves, doubtful of this facileness of Santrisen's.

The High Police Priest is not sure whether he's

impressed. He looks over at the Police Commander, who looks back impassively and stays silent. The High Priest sighs, "The plan seems too easy for such a formidably disruptive beast."

Santrisen smiles. "That's right, sire." He thinks back and smiles some more to himself. "But, you see, that's just how money works. In those worlds, the story is always the same: that the creators of money— sooner or later—become absolute rulers of their worlds. Which is the needed prelude for their getting nullified."

"Do you mean to—?"

"That's right. They are allowed to get all the money power in the world and then find out they really have nothing; or rather they know it all along—it's part of their plan—but finally they *understand* it."

"So of course they can't deal with this."

"That's right. They can rule some things and everything. But not nothing. It's as though all the death blows of the aeons hit them back almost at once. This is called 'Payback.' To sum up, money only appears to exist, and appears to get things, but in verity is understood to get, and be, nothing once people stop believing in it. The greatest money holders are, from then, the most voided. So, by giving this creature the supply of all money, he should be undone with exquisite ease.

To my judgment, it is the finest way to make it stop being."

The High Priest of Police stands up and smiles broadly, which looks strange on his normally serious face. "Santrisen, you tickle me chartreuse! Money starts feeling like a weapon. Commandino, have an agency calculate the 'monetary value' for everything that exists in the Empire, coin a money symbol, and we shall leave the Monster an offering at that sum. When we move this beast to accept tribute, it shall be no more!"

V

A dissenting faction of agents doesn't square with Santrisen's plan, and discretely agrees to slip out of the meeting to cultivate an alternative.

"Or an altar native," quips one.

"By which you allude to Vatvoy?" asks a colleague.

"Truly," responds the first. "If all four of us have one thing in common (4=1), it's that we don't abide by this Santrisen upstart's idea. But I believe we can gain from Vatvoy's counsel."

A third agent nods. "Santrisen, he comes in and tells us what to do. He says he knows money, which, by the by, doesn't exist. So he knows lots and lots about nothing. Splendid! Thank you, Santrisen, but you're not welcome!"

The fourth agent is quiet and pensive, and then interjects. "I don't like his name."

Laughing, the first agent adds, "I don't like his face. Doesn't reflect my truths back nearly enough. So how can I work with him?"

The four agents make way on their powered roller boots for Vatvoy's lair, which lies in a mountainous cave outside the Imperial City. As they ride on the glass-smooth road, in row formation, they clearly hear the Monster's pronouncements and see his vast display of apparent lights. They shrug and nod to one another. As agents, their nerves are sturdier than most citizens', many of whom stand or amble about idly and aimlessly, harangued by the infrasensory onslaught. The slaves, however, move about as usual, most not even aware of the Monster's presence.

As they reach the mountainous region of country, they slide off the road and onto the rocky grass. The third agent points to a craggy grey-blue rock formation and says, "Up there is where we go."

After considerable climbing adventures, they reach the right plateau and spot a massive cave entrance. There is no gate, door, or barrier of any kind. "Do we just walk in?" asks the second agent.

"Yes, of course, please do. Please come in," entreats Vatvoy, waving them in rather insistently.

The agents take a slight fright over their host's sudden appearance among them, but he quickly sets them at ease with his friendly comments: "You know, my door is always open. I want everyone to visit me, at least once each. But he or she sometimes doesn't. My door isn't there at all. Or maybe it is, because my guests sometimes get shut out, according to their opinion. It may be an invisible forcefield made of their very little desire!"

The second agent exhales and gets to the point. "Great Vatvoy, we need your help with that vast hellion that mocks sound and light. . . . What can be done? The Temple's plan to use the money is a weak experiment at best." The agents share the plan's key points. Vatvoy ponders, and replies, "A weak experiment? That feels nice to me." He positions himself cross-legged on a boulder and caresses a one-petalled daisy growing out of a crack in the rock. "But, oh, what they're doing is a strong experiment, which is why it may not like to work. No, no!"

The four agents look at each other, mildly surprised to find some confirmation they were possibly right about the plan. The first agent asks, "Vatvoy, what is it about the Monster that Santrisen's plan won't work on it?"

"You tell me to tell you. Actually . . . heh . . . the Monster squirrels away anything it's given. Even if it's worth squatdown! It holds on to it forever in the hope that some day its value will be high! If the Temple thinks this Squirrel will be swayed to nil by the secret nothingness, it is thinking all wrong strong!"

"Then the gift of money can not dislodge or destructure the Monster?" asks the first agent.

Vatvoy looks directly at the first agent. "Of course not! To the Squirrel Monster, waiting there for all time is easy. Loves waiting because it loves time. Squirrel believes time *is* money."

The fourth agent is puzzled. "So then why does it . . . ?"

Vatvoy answers, "Because it wants *more*. All of precious time-money is not enough. The Squirrel collects! It takes, takes, takes. Shakes, shakes, shakes." Vatvoy laughs to himself.

The second agent looks uncertain. "So what are we to do? It must want something enough to leave."

Vatvoy raises an eyebrow and lightly grins. "O hero! What are you *not* to do? Do you consider it? Go the whole way. If you review all the things you are not to do, then by elimination you know what to do!"

The second through fourth agents are displeased at

this counsel, and unwittingly make faces with their energy.

Vatvoy continues. "Yes! No one likes thinking backward. And yet . . . you use those roller tootsie booties to go in reverse, do you not? Do you? Ah, yeah way!"

The first agent smiles.

"You there," says Vatvoy, "Your smile is a badge of honor in this drought. It touches my own cheeks. Stay a while, while these other boys go skating back many a mile."

Facing an exceptional invitation by so great a personage as Vatvoy, the agent does nothing but agree. The others, knowing that their audience with the Grand Nothingness is suddenly expiring, bow tensely, turn on their heels, and walk out.

Vatvoy looks at the first agent. "You hear that? The attitude? They took it personal about their booties. And what for? I think the little wheels are rather fetching."

The first agent laughs heartily. Vatvoy beams.

VI

A police captain wearing the traditional police captain's dress uniform—featuring a waist-length black cape and a wide-brimmed black hat—arrives at the Monster's chosen rendezvous, namely the Fountain Mountain in the middle of Eternity Nau Park, to lay the prize on the valley lawn as demanded by the beast in his recent pronouncements. The discordant whine-moans are phasing into calmer refrains, lulled—maybe—in anticipation of the expected ransom. Their vague translation is "Yes, money, yes."

Removing the cherished universal fortune from a velvet purse, the captain places a coin made of engraved wood (spruce bred with ebony) on the ground, and lets out a sigh. Under his breath, he mutters, "Would that I could crush this piece beneath my high-heeled boot." He takes a few steps back. The Monster's intelligence mechanically zones in on the unique coin and coolly absorbs it from his position on the horizon, seemingly aware that the space between him and anything he deals with isn't really there. The infinite riches taken thusly by the vast monstrous entity, the captain turns around and slowly walks off.

The Monster continues with his screams, harangues and groans, except they don't translate anymore as they reach people's ears.

VII

Hereta is at her girlfriend Safrette's house. The Monster's aweful bleatings race across the land and sky. "There's a rhythm in there somewhere," says Safrette about them, while casually leafing through the latest edition of the *Book of Idols,* which displays and describes the crop of musicians who currently hold power over the slaves' imaginations. She laughs. "What if the Monster becomes the most prominent star in the cosmic iconography? What if everyone begins to love the flow of his hidden beats and melodies, including the free people?"

Hereta smiles from Safrette's bed, as she paints her toenails a compound of gold and lapis lazuli. "Or free people only. He doesn't reach the slaves at all, you know."

"Well, sure. Slaves favor this really obvious musical ritual," referring to the book's contents. "Feel what you think about this one. 'Fabido Tigerman. His specialty is smiling with his tongue sticking out.'"

Watching the paint quickly dry on her nails, Hereta feels a new idea set coming on. "I mean, just listen to it. It's almost like there's no true sound at all. I don't get any visions. There's a total lack of real color, wouldn't you say?"

Safrette, somewhat sharing in the growing idea set, responds, "Yes . . . it doesn't give anything. Maybe it doesn't have stuffs to give."

Hereta wraps up her thought. "It doesn't offer things to dip into. Come on, let's go outside and dance!"

They step out onto the courtyard in front of Safrette's house. Though there is almost no wind, the clouds in the evening sky float about in strange courses, as if confused by the Monster's epic sonic whines.

Hereta is barefoot but Safrette is wearing high-heeled silver sandals. Hereta puts her hair up in a bun and decides to keep her little purse necklace on. She faces Safrette and they clasp their hands together. They begin swaying and moving to the staccato cacophony of the Monster's growled rants. They then let go and, always in synch, pirouette and twirl and dip, in this way and that. They bow, then curtsy, then raise their arms up, letting the sounds guide them. Hereta reaches into her purse necklace, takes out her compact mirror, and points the surface in the Monster's direction. It reflects back a slender green beam to the monstrous horizon, apparently refracted out of nowhere.

"The middle color. The color of the heart!" Hereta

cries out, stopping the dance.

"Oh, my. . . ." says Safrette warmly.

VIII

The mood at the Police Council feels glum and more than a little exasperated. With Santrisen's plan proven a likely dud, no one is initiating bold or vigorous proposals. Doubt lingers through the aether.

Although embarrassment is a suspect emotion to the High Police Priest, he does feel some discomfort. "Santrisen, you have come out a dude dud."

"Giving contrition, excellency," Santrisen offers with a bow.

"Fine. Carry yourself out. This is a strange affair for us all," the High Priest says, gripping his armrests. Santrisen leaves.

An agent slowly stands with a certain sufficient confidence. "Instead of everything which is really nothing, can we give this Monster something? To satiate him? Make him go away?"

"I think not," the High Priest responds curtly. "His voraciousness is a vortex. He wants all."

The agent thinks aloud as a new idea escapes his lips. "What if everything, nothing, and something are the same to him?"

A chill goes through the long chamber, as the speculation pointedly sinks its talons in. It implies the Monster's eternal presence. No deal possible, no way out.

Stiff silence ensues. But the High Priest notes to himself the Police Commander's suede-smooth calm. Evenly, he sets a new ball rolling. "Does anyone else have a plan?"

A young agent rises to speak. "I went with three companions earlier today to ask Vatvoy for assistance and, after they left, had a private interview."

The High Priest frowns but maintains connection. "What did he say?"

"He said my right arm was too hairy. He refused to speak with me further unless I completely shaved my right arm."

The High Priest's eyes look moist, glistening. "What did you do?"

"I went out, grabbed hold of a sharp-edged rock, shaved it, and returned."

"And then?"

"He said I wasn't assertive enough, that because I hadn't insisted that he speak with me immediately, I must not consider this Squirrel to be so important or menacing. And thus he couldn't be bothered to help the Council 'put on its pajamas' or 'bake distilled tidbits.'"

"Squirrel? Is that what he calls the Monster?" the High Priest smiles sardonically with light disbelief.

"By the Reality of the Realm, he is mad, glad, and bad!!" spits one councilor.

"Shixcrement!" yells another, pounding a chubby fist on the massive table.

At this moment, an apparition of gold, silver, grey, and white light appears floating above the Council's meeting table, emitting a pleasant humming noise. Soon the light and noise coalesce into a talking image of Vatvoy. "Ah, but someone has uttered one of my Holy Words. How very cute. Unlike, say, carnivorous bunnies. Gentlemen, I implore you: feel stress. This isn't me but a projection, which, by the way, is being cast in all wave spectra. Consider it more real than me. I'm even considering killing myself instead of ever turning it off."

"Vatvoy, you play with our minds!" a council member cries out.

"Which is especially unacceptable during times of urgency!" charges another.

"Re-read your schoolbooks, council members. Life is a comedy-drama."

At this, the council members suddenly become calm.

Vatvoy's image turns, with eyes blazing and voice soft, to the slightly raised throne at the head of the Council's table. "I charge you, High Priest, with not knowing how to deal with the Squirrel."

The High Priest remains composed, knowing there is a long-standing, if subtle, rivalry between he and Vatvoy.

Vatvoy's image intones further. "While you aren't imperial, as dictator it is your duty to dictate generalized life chunks that nourish wisdom. And in this you come across negligient. Well, I seem to think so, at any rate."

A few councilors, and the Police Commander, raise an eyebrow.

"But who has time for such petty trivia? A trick question, on at least four levels. You there, with the blue hat, what's so funny? In truth, to keep this Council weak, I've come to give you the solution or antidote, if you will, to the Squirrel, who is a monster from the ancient days of humoneyty or humanity. For in that era and area, there are two principal sayings: first, and most sublime, 'Dog is man's best friend' and, second, 'Diamonds are a girl's best friend.' As long as people persist in these sayings, they are split in twain, as though at war or in any conflict. For loyalty is polarized as against luxury, tenderness as against hardness, obedience against opulence, and so on. Only when a third saying, 'Diamond Dogs are my best friend,' is uttered do beauty and truth hold sway. The exaltation of the world follows from this, indeed, is it. The temporal realm of the ancients and the eternal realm of the moderns get conjoined, and it's fun."

"By Mana Labara! Never has Vatvoy sounded forth with such coherence!" exclaims a councilor.

"Yes, but this is a projection," responds another.

"The point misses you," retorts the first.

Vatvoy's image smiles. "Gents, you burn with ardor kindling to express impulse particles, talk all at once, and unwrap problem swaths so the solution mark comes out clean and shiny. But you strain much. Oh so much. You make efforts but don't have efforts make *you*. Any questions?"

"He doesn't understand your projection stance, Vatvoy," offers the first councilor.

Vatvoy's projection picks its teeth with a tiny ivory scimitar. "Yes, you call the projection 'Vatvoy' and I now step out." Vatvoy's image becomes Vatvoy, who hops onto the Police Council's table and stomps on it twice with one of his gargantuan dust-covered boots, as if saying *I'm in the flesh* but also *I'm alert to your minutes-taking ways.*

The Council offers its attention, and Vatvoy speaks

plainly. "To vanquish the Squirrel, you must go to the Park and speak the word Di-Do. Upon receiving this, the Monster's own archaic agony memories will unlock and render him noble. You should say it, but also spray it from within your rooster. This is key. Diamond jam with tiny puppies. Or pearl jelly with tiny guppies!"

And, with that, Vatvoy is suddenly not there, though no one seems to have noticed how he left.

Oh, one of the agents was sent to the Park to carry out this recipe, soon after which the Squirrel monster or manster budged, appeared to smile wistfully, and left the universal sphere with a grateful air. The agent chosen by the High Priest was Santrisen, perhaps to punish him for the previous failure of his plan. But if this was the case, the High Priest erred in his calculus; for this mission turned out to be Santrisen's vindication, both within himself as well as in the people's estimation of him as a hero.

Aeons later, when asked about the incident, Vatvoy replied, "Santrisen and I are one and the same. He is me, and I am him. The High Priest didn't realize he volunteered me to carry out my own recipe."